Am[illegible]
Blanket

Written by Jillian Powell

Illustrated by Sarah Warburton

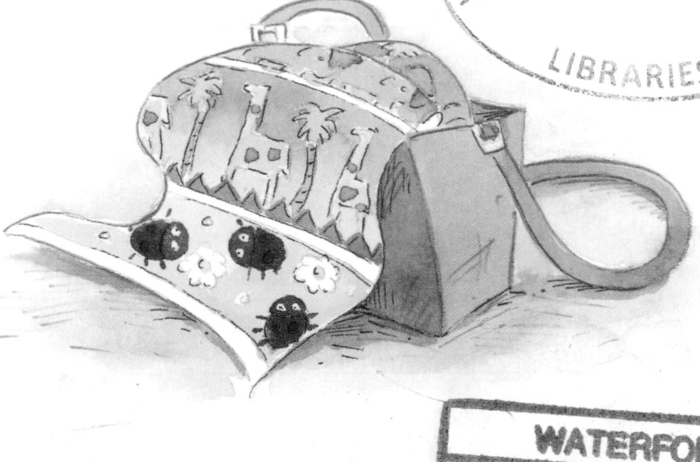

What is in Ama's bag?

What is it?

It is a cloak.

What is it?

It is a flag.

What is it?

It is a rug.

What is it?
Under the Sea
Ellie
Matt
Ama

It is a bag.
Home
Adventures

What is it?
Aladdin

It is a magic carpet.

What is it?

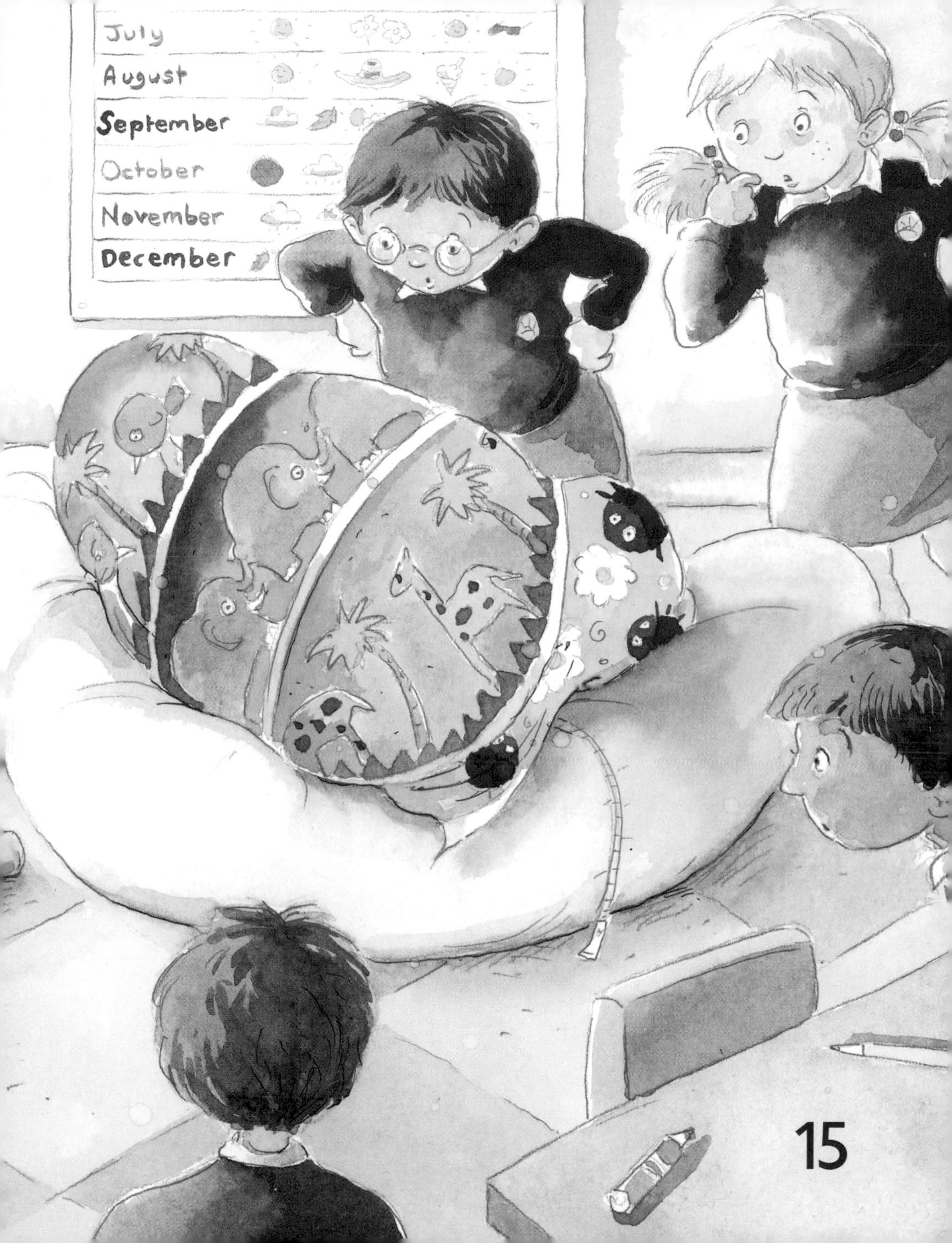
July
August
September
October
November
December

It is a special blanket.

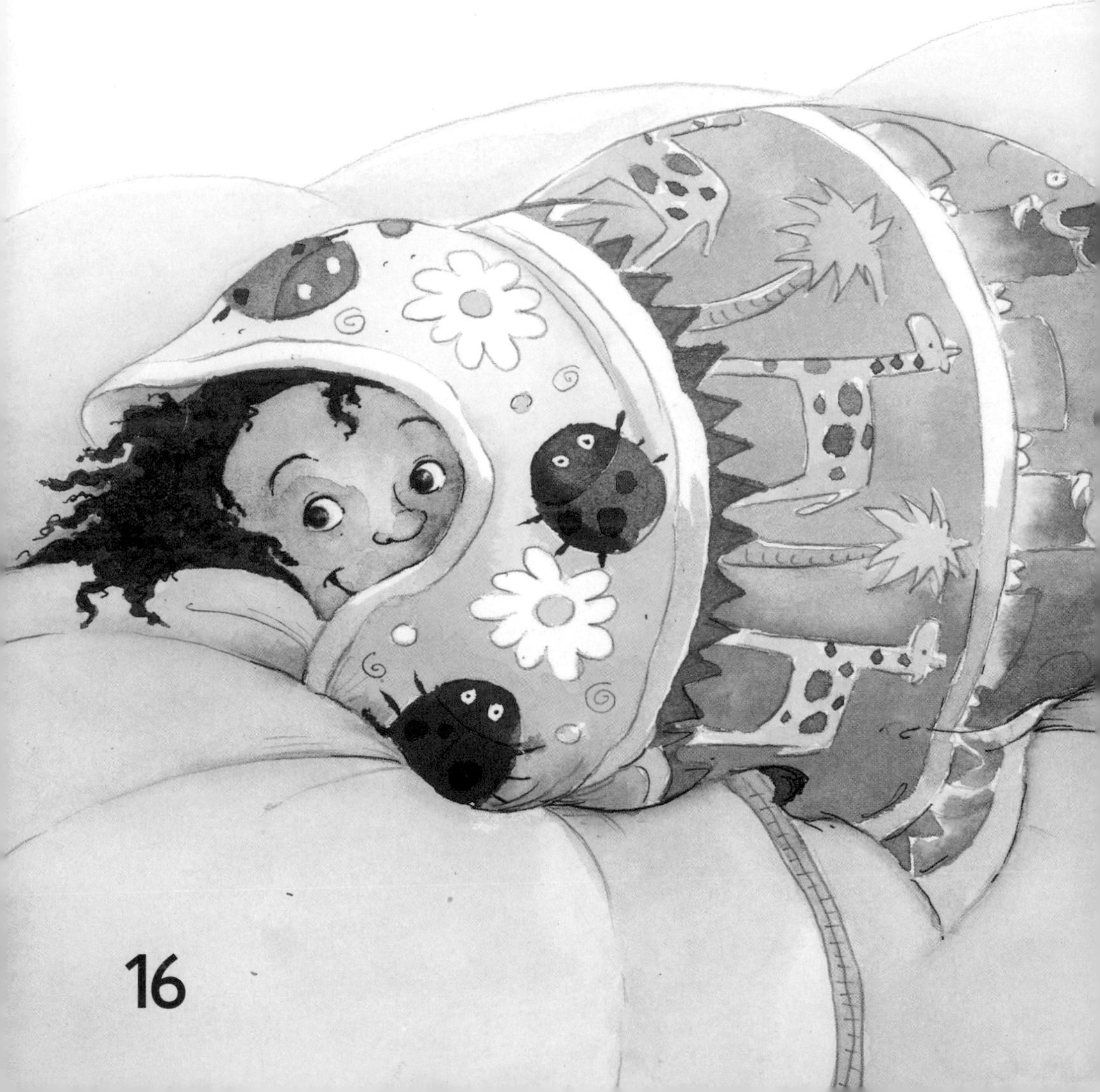